CHICK & CHICKIE

PLAY ALL DAY!

AAAH!

A TOON BOOK BY

Claude Ponti

For Adèle

Editorial Director: FRANÇOISE MOULY

Book Design: JONATHAN BENNETT & FRANÇOISE MOULY

CLAUDE PONTI'S artwork was done in ink and watercolors.

A TOON Book™ © 2012 RAW Junior, LLC, 27 Greene Street, New York, NY 10013. Original text and illustrations from *Tromboline et Foulbazar: les masques* and *Tromboline et Foulbazar: le A*, © 1995 & 1998 l'école des loisirs, Paris. Translation and TOON Book™ edition © 2012 RAW Junior, LLC. TOON Books®, TOON Graphics™, LITTLE LIT® and TOON Into Reading™ are trademarks of RAW Junior, LLC. All rights reserved. No part of this book may be used or reproduced in any manner whatsoever without written permission except in the case of brief quotations embodied in critical articles and reviews. All our books are Smyth Sewn (the highest library-quality binding available) and printed with soy-based inks on acid-free, woodfree paper harvested from responsible sources. Printed in China by C&C Offset Printing Co., Ltd. TOON Books are distributed by Consortium Book Sales & Distribution, a division of Ingram Content Group; orders (866) 400-5351; ips@ingramcontent.com; www.cbsd.com.

The Library of Congress has cataloged the hardcover edition as follows:
Ponti, Claude, 1948-   Chick & Chickie play all day! / by Claude Ponti   p. cm. "A TOON book."   Based on two of the author's books, previously published in French: *Tromboline et Foulbazar: les masques*, and *Tromboline et Foulbazar: le A*. Summary: Two young chicks have fun making masks and playing with the letter A. ISBN: 978-1-935179-14-6 (hardcover) 1. Graphic novels. [1. Graphic novels. 2. Chickens–Fiction. 3. Play–Fiction.] I. Title. II. Title: Chick and Chickie play all day! PZ7.7.P66Ch 2012 741.5'944--dc23   2011026764

ISBN: 978-1-935179-29-0
18 19 20 21 22 23 C&C 10 9 8 7 6 5 4

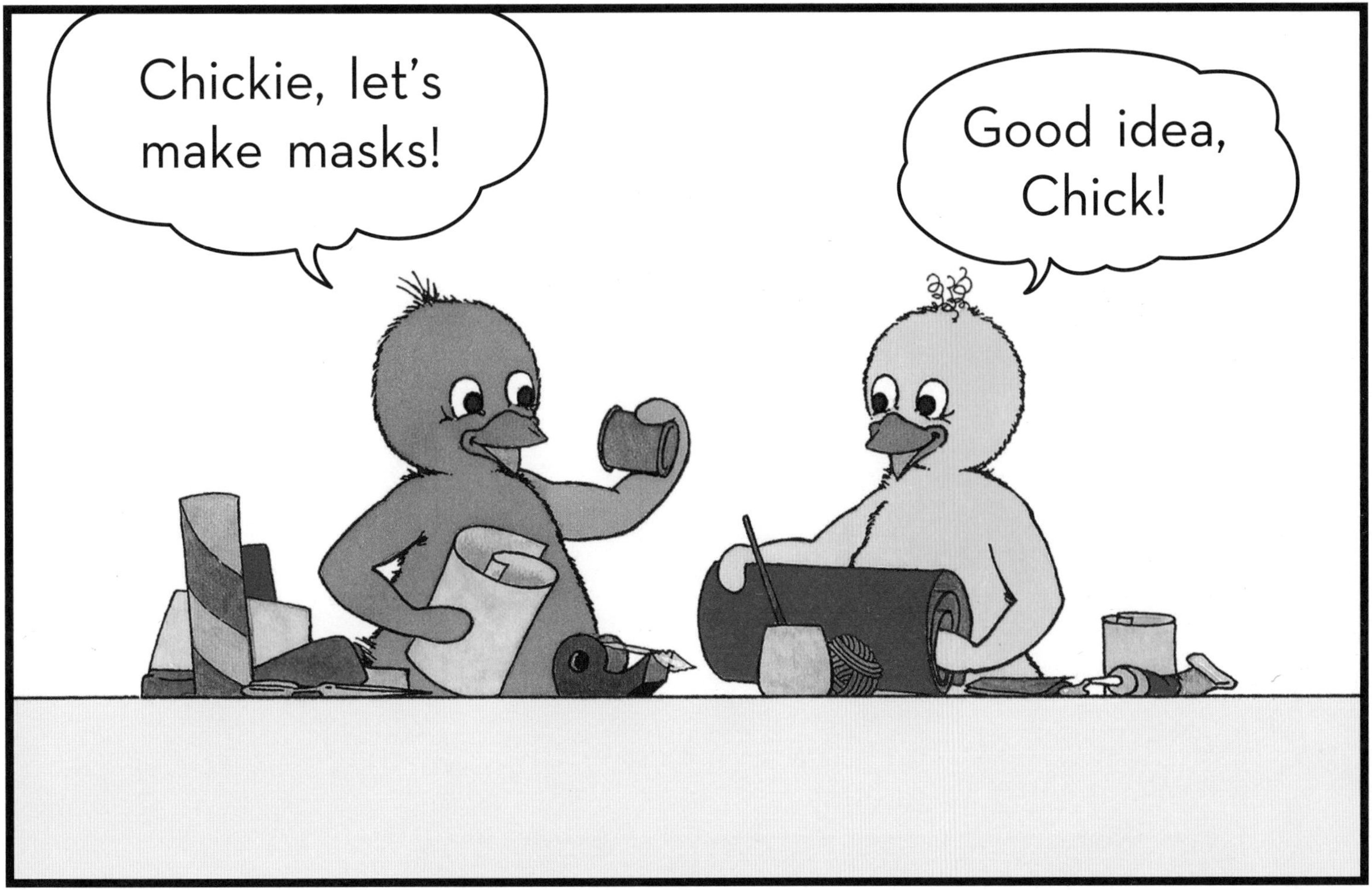
Chickie, let's make masks!
Good idea, Chick!

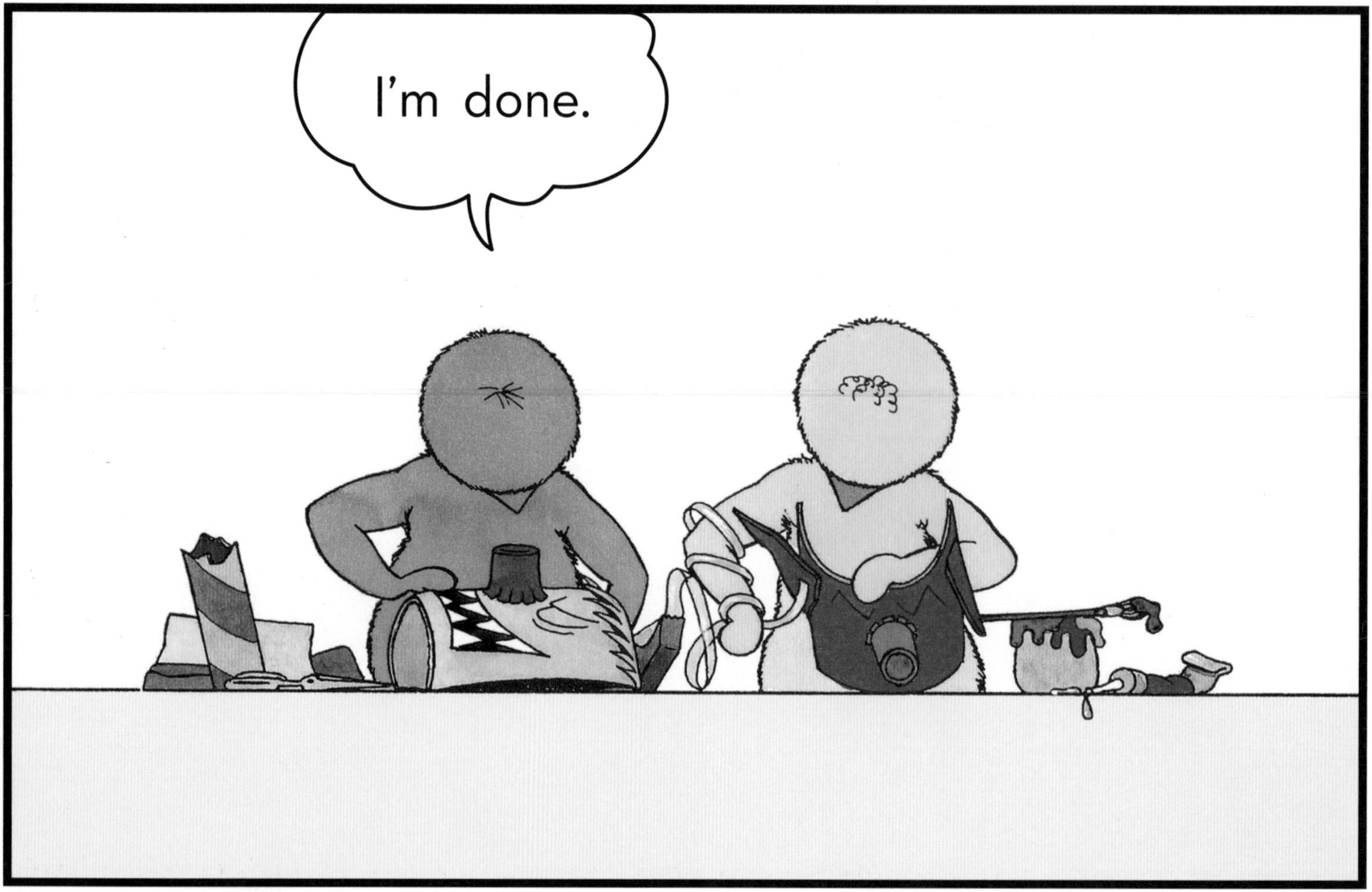
I’m done.

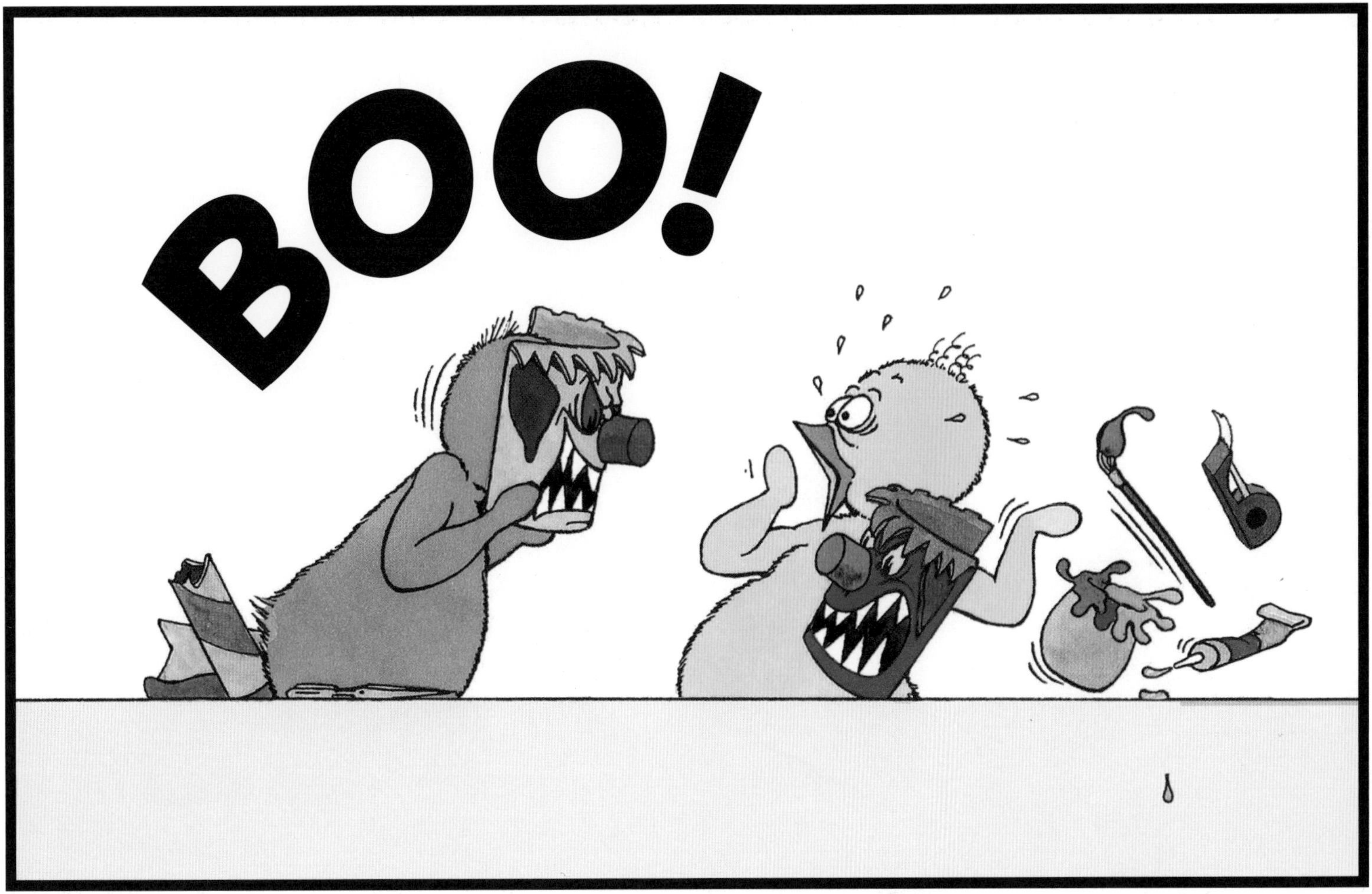
BOO!

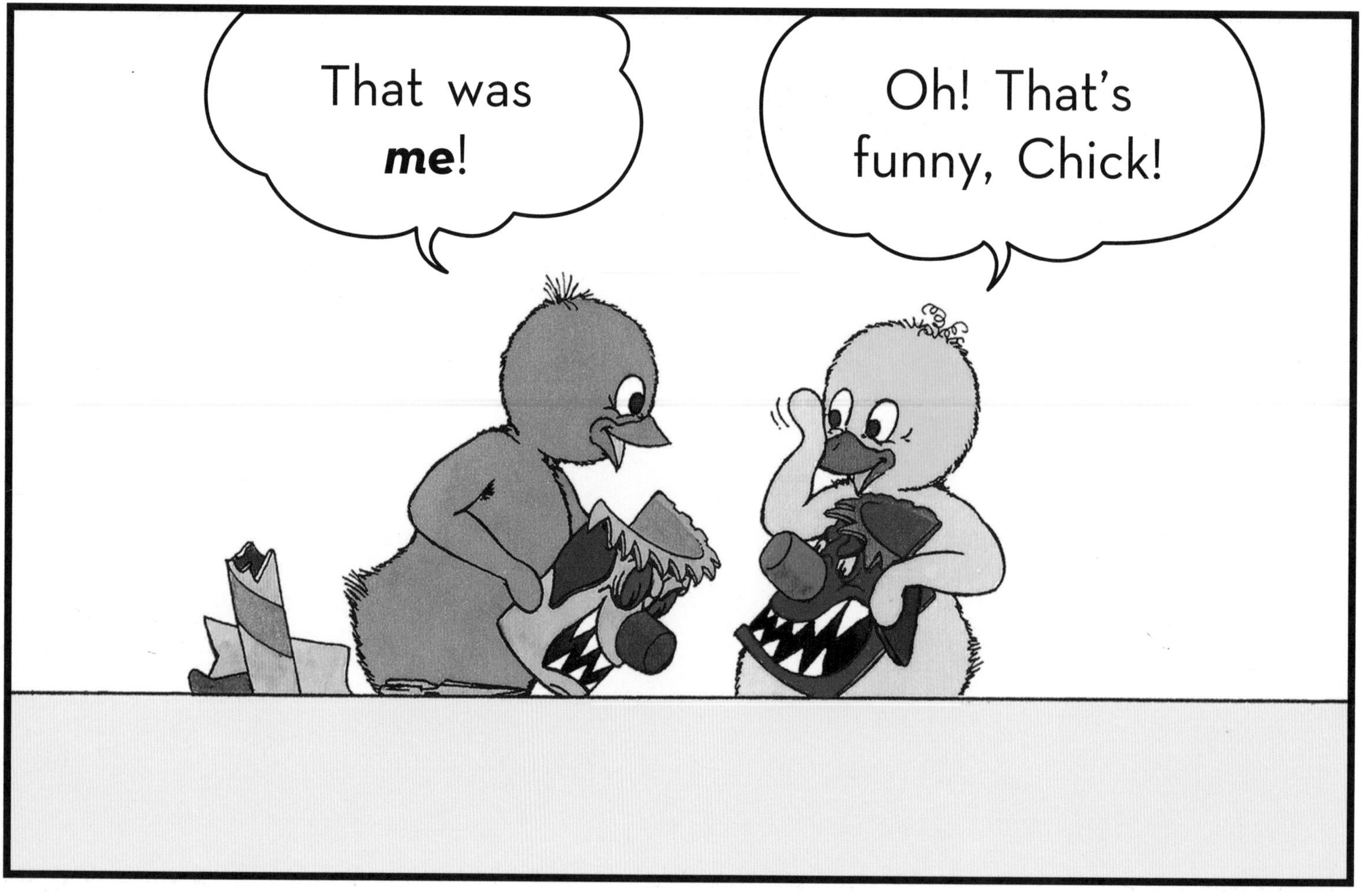
That was ***me***!
Oh! That's funny, Chick!

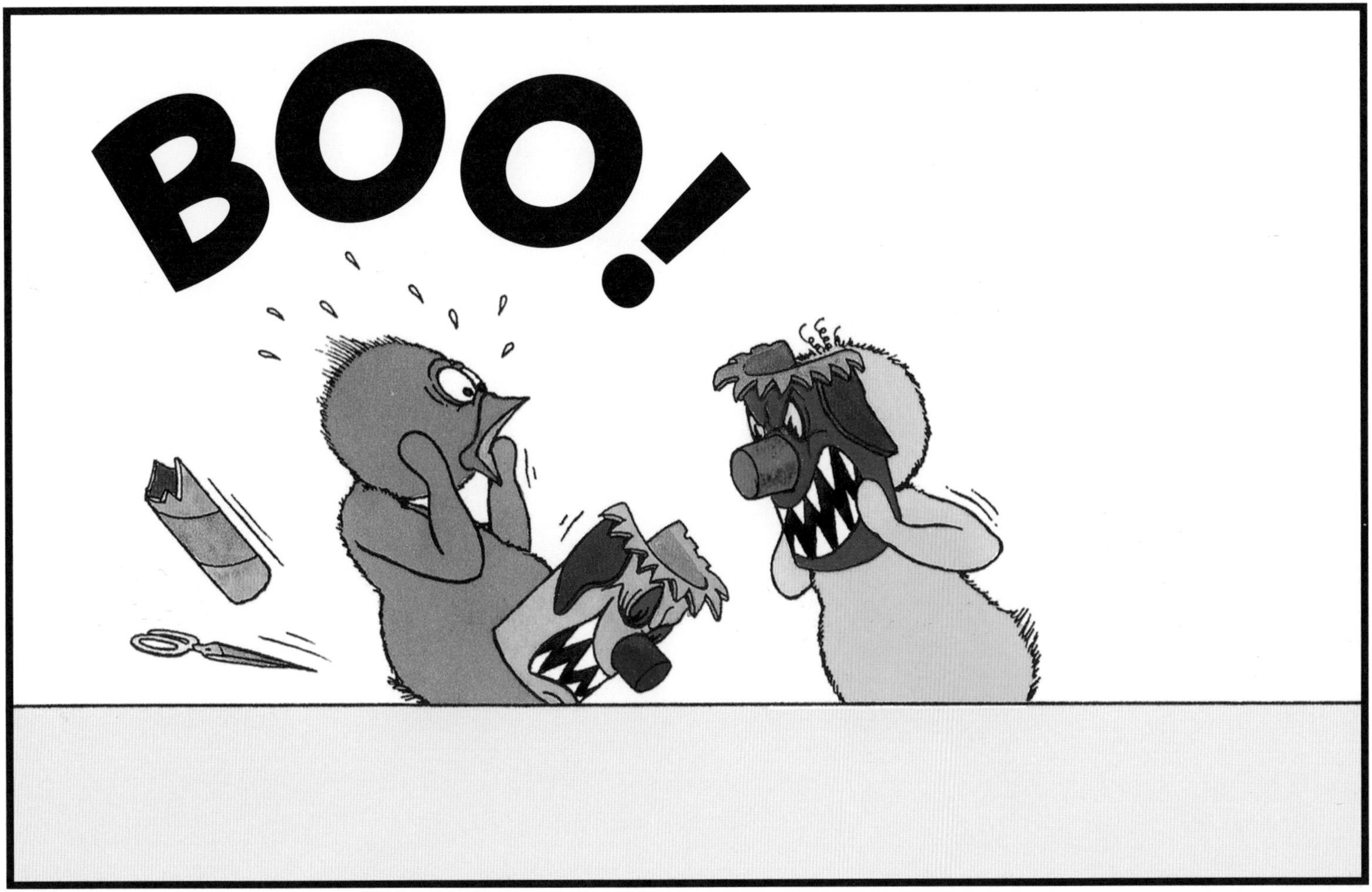
BOO!

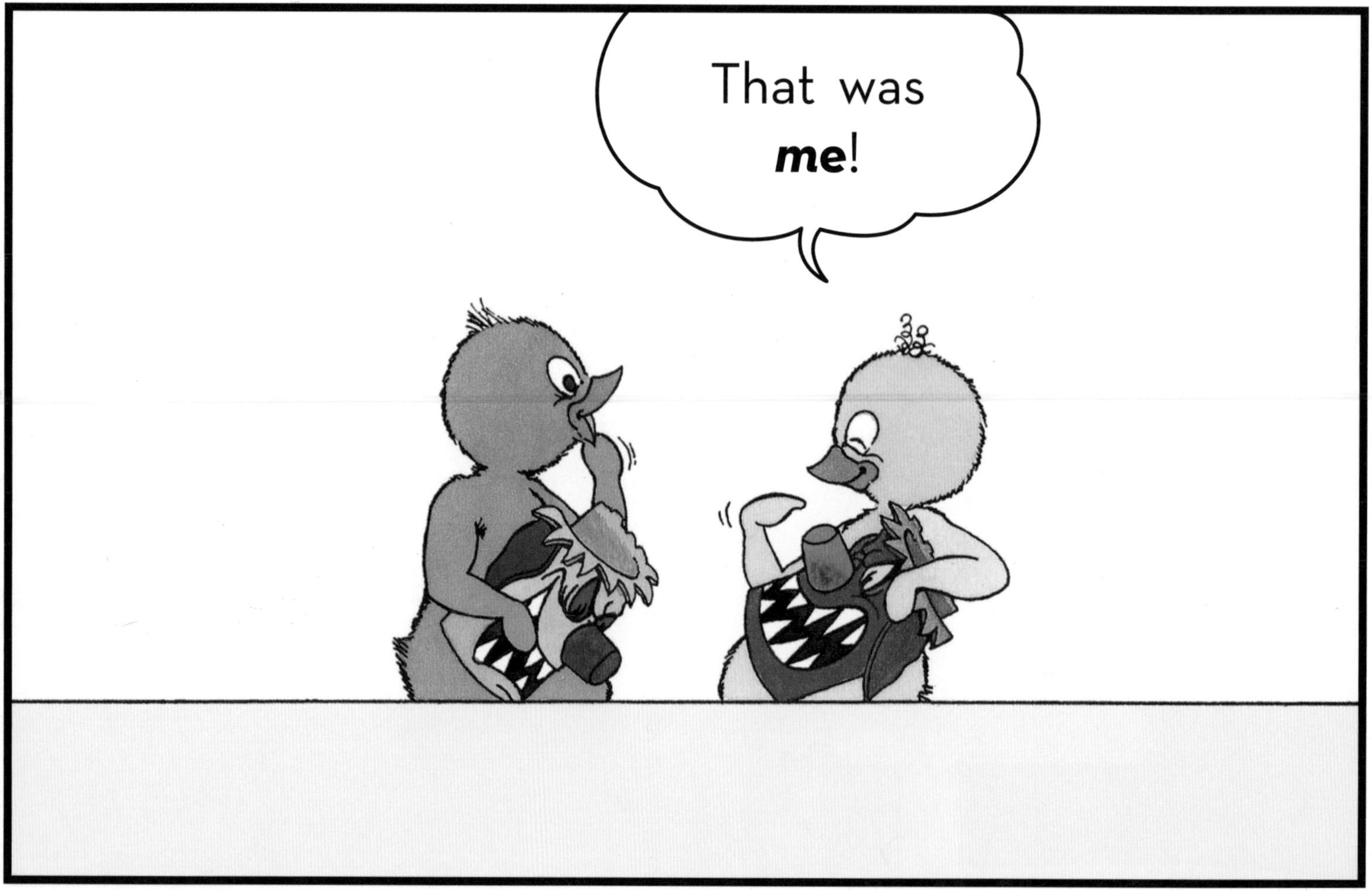
That was ***me***!

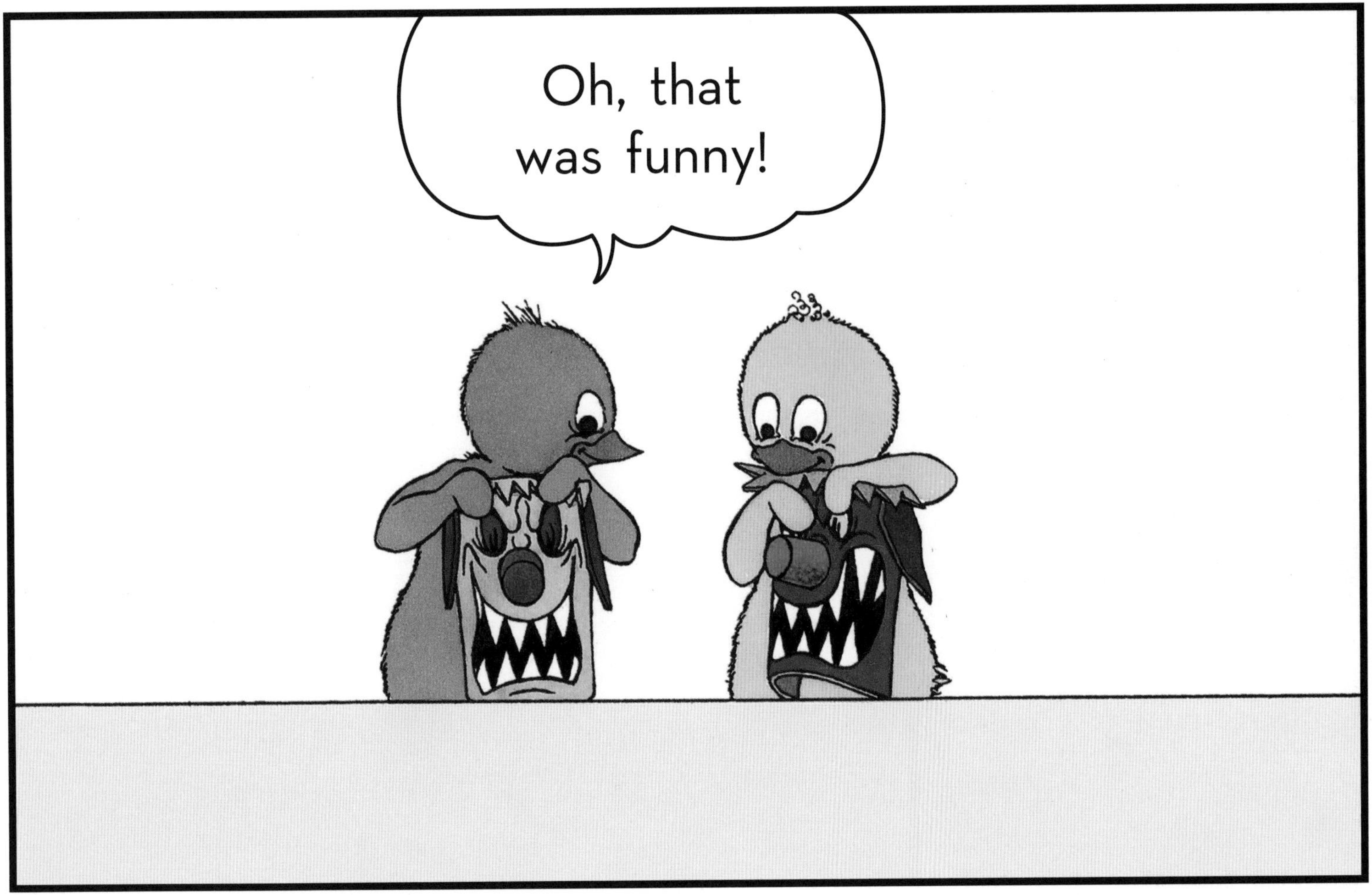
Oh, that was funny!

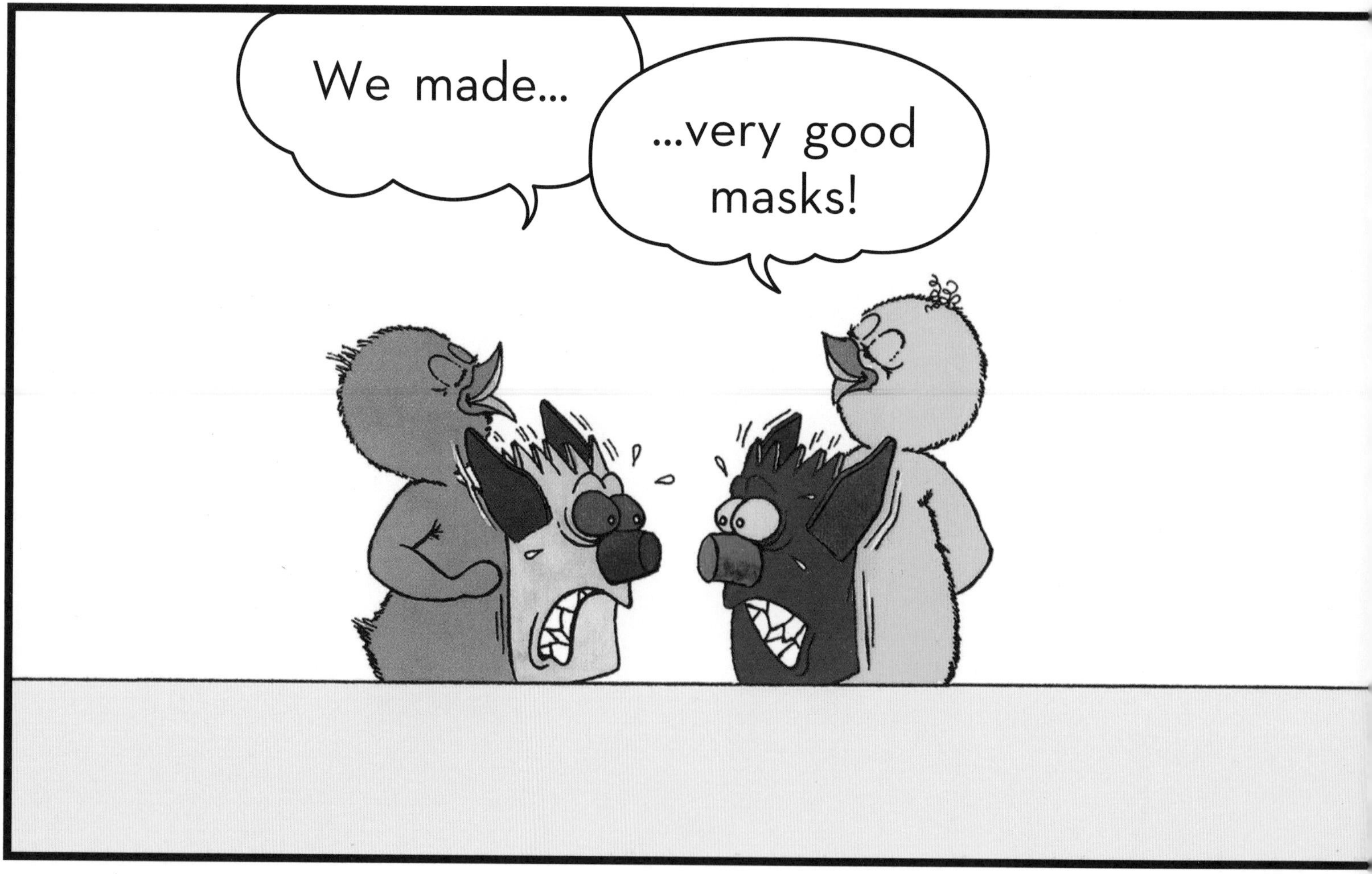
We made...
...very good masks!

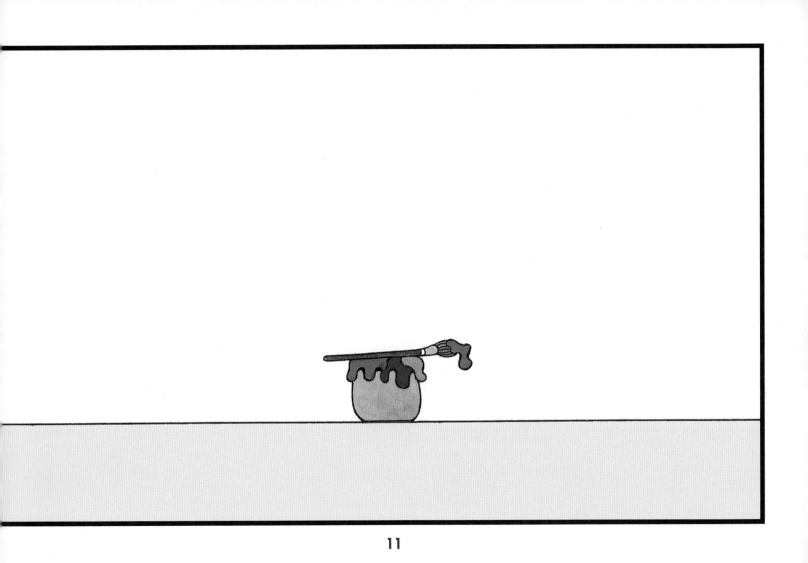

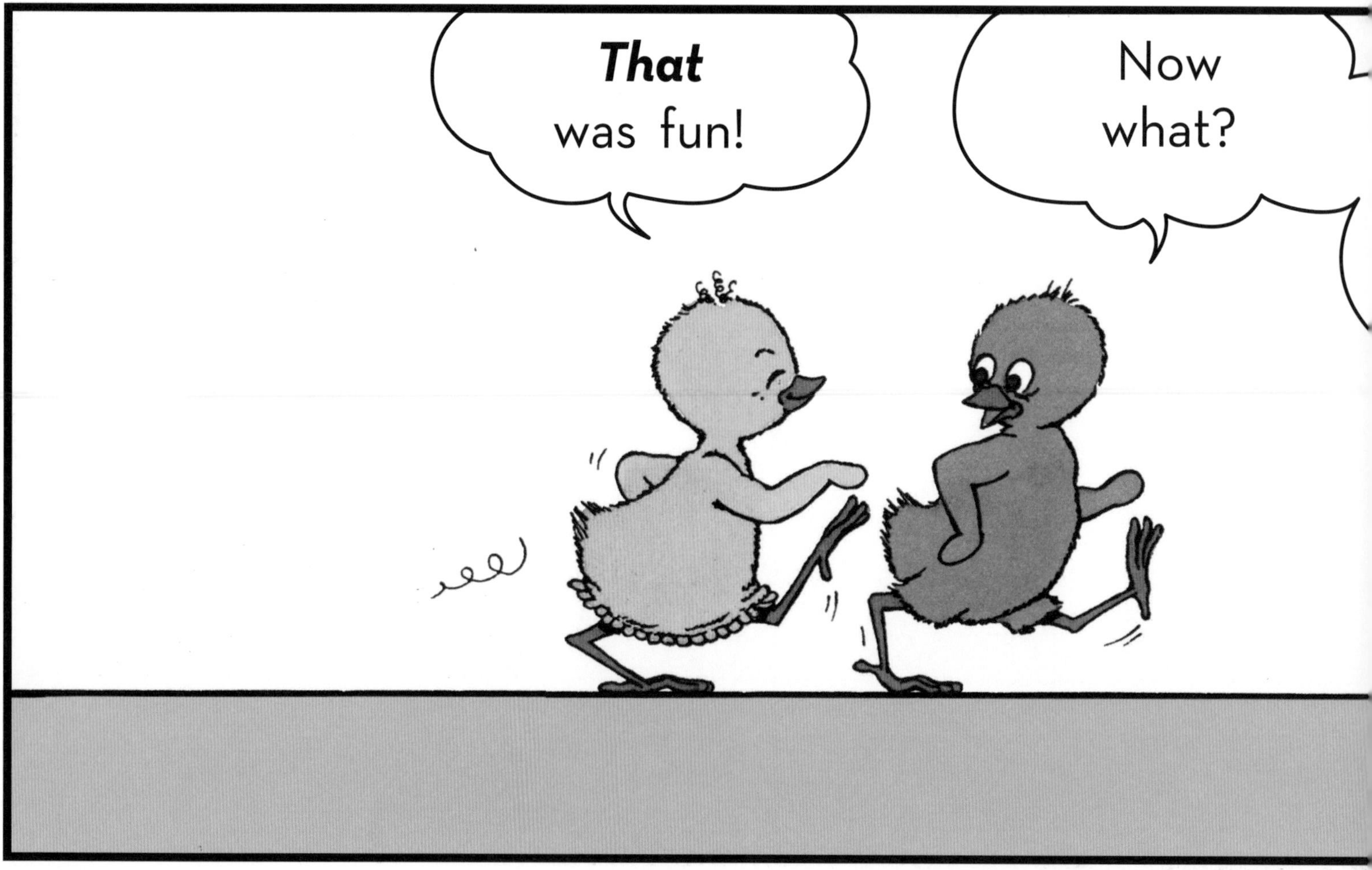
That was fun!
Now what?

What do **you** want to do?

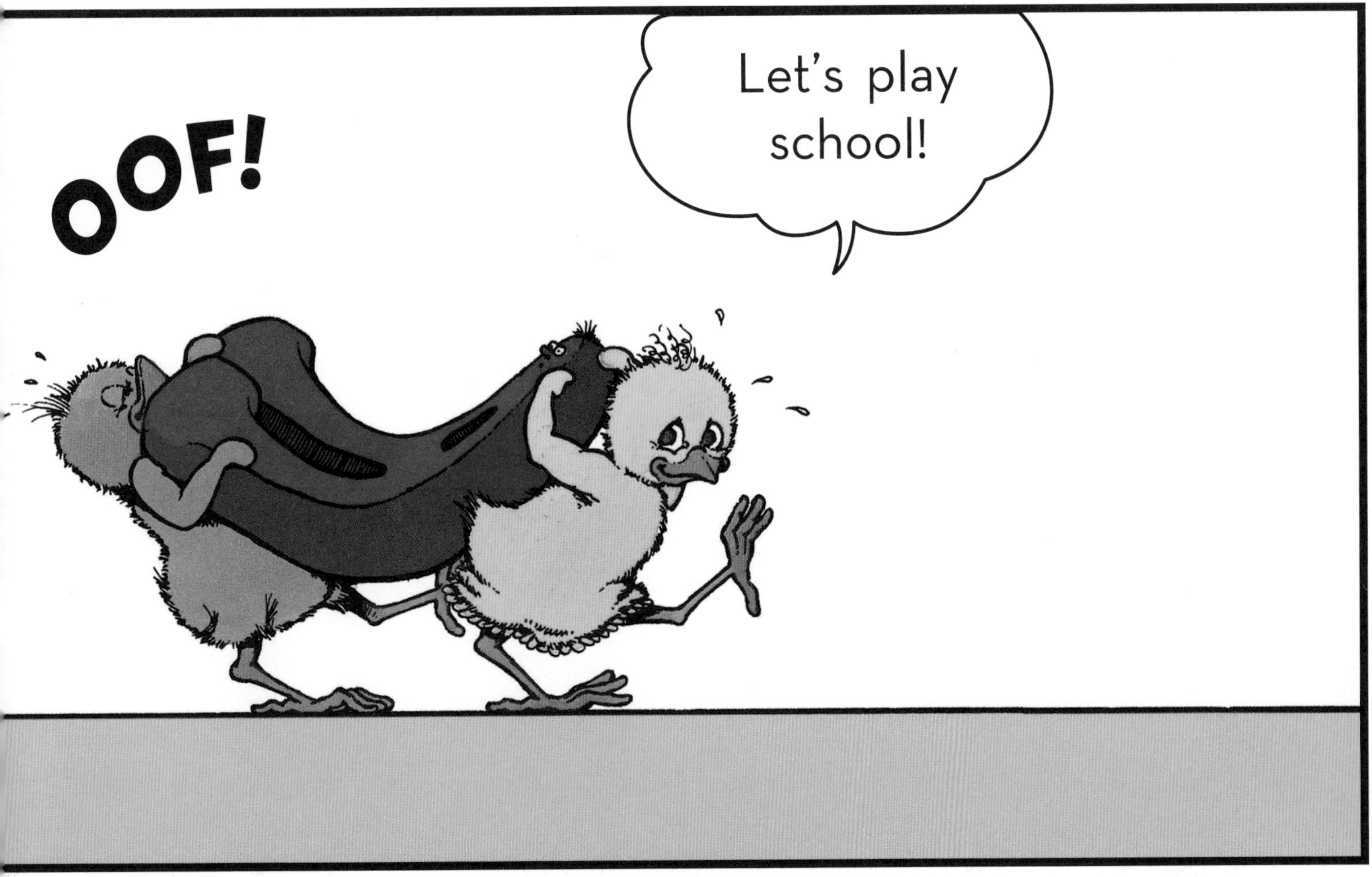
OOF!
Let's play school!

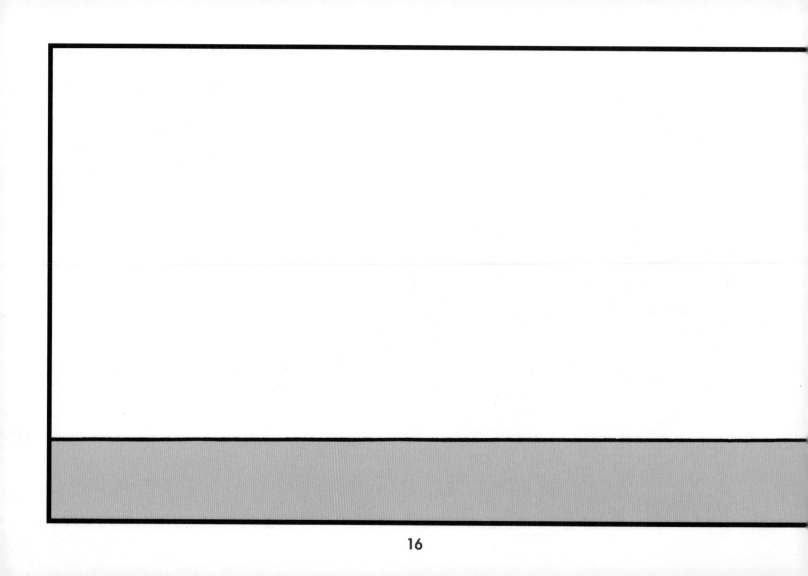

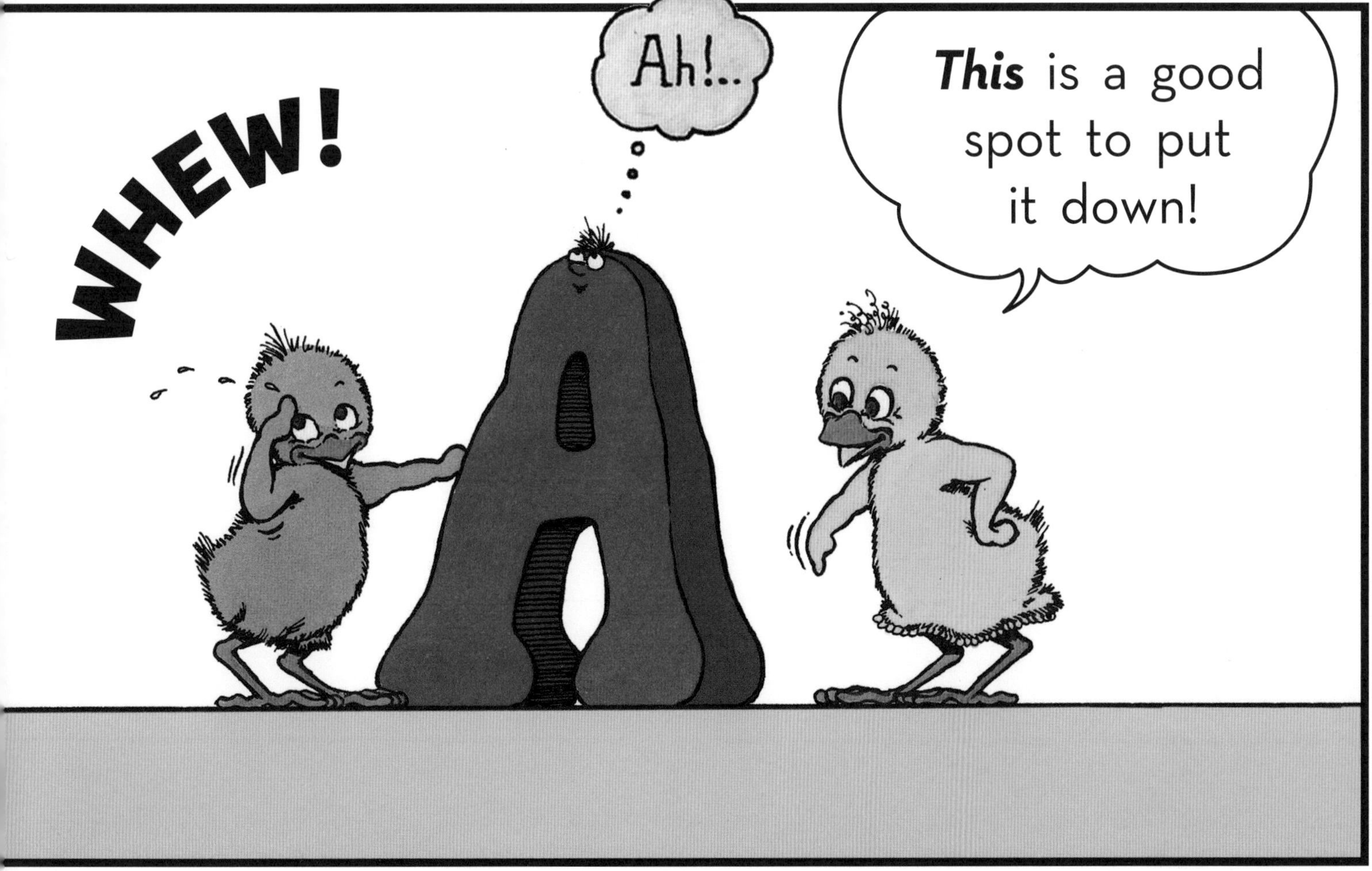
WHEW!
Ah!..
This is a good spot to put it down!

When we ***tickle*** the A...

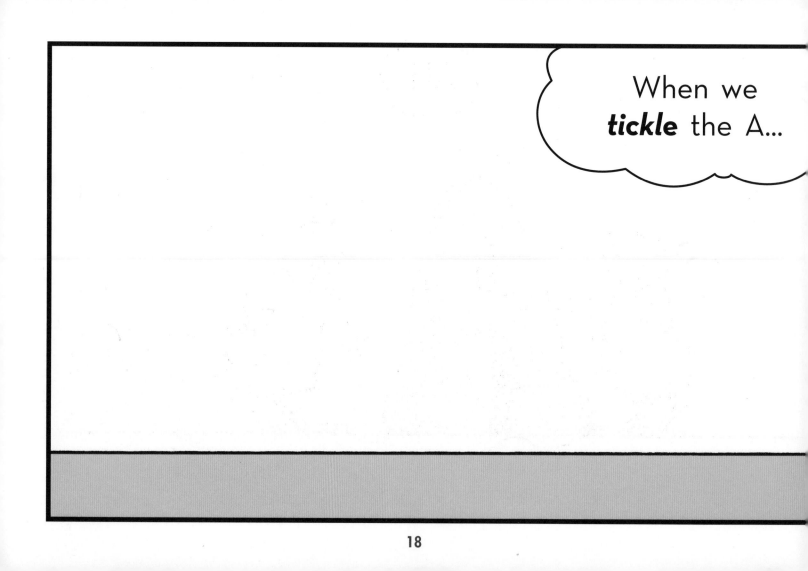

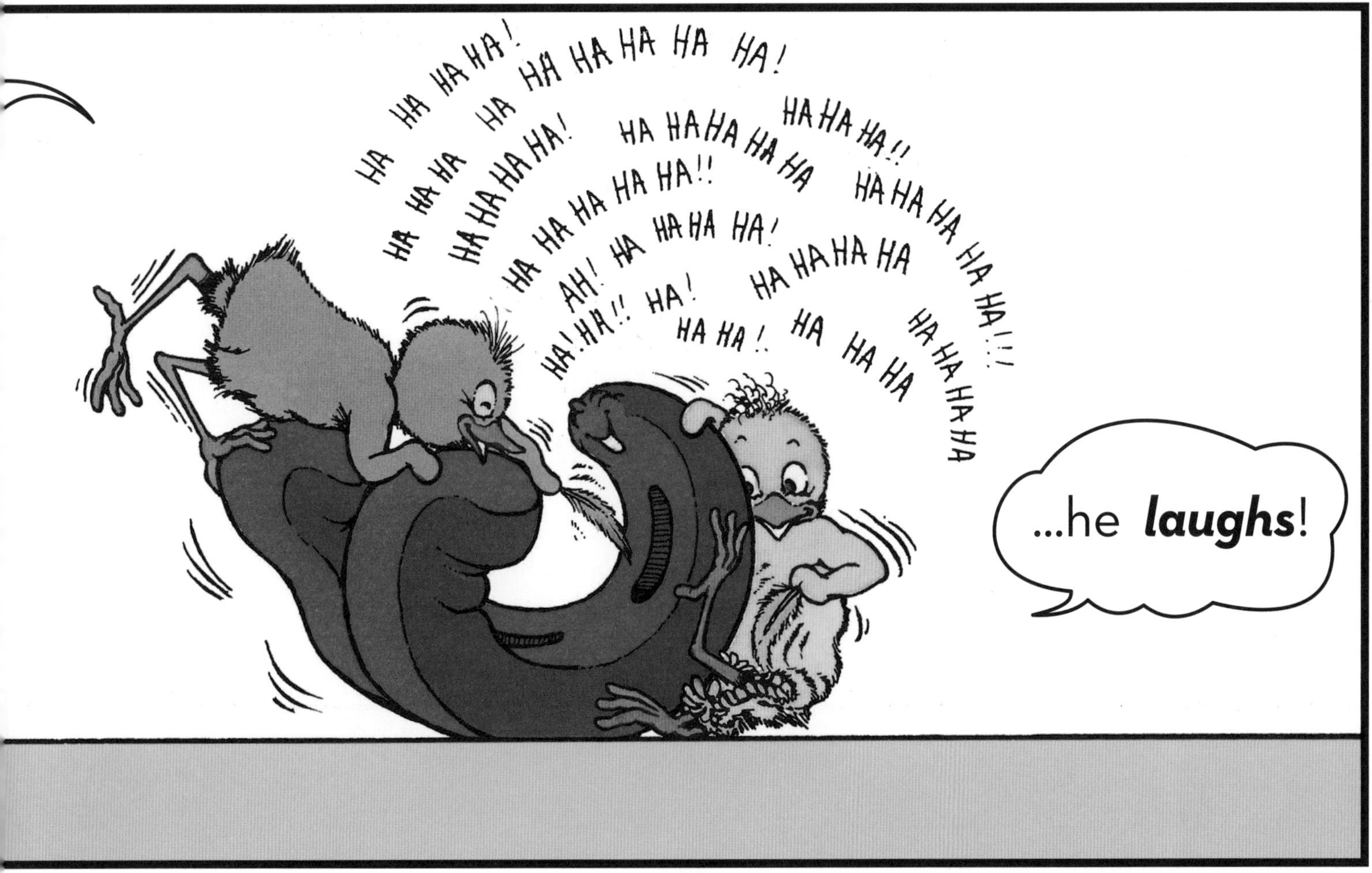

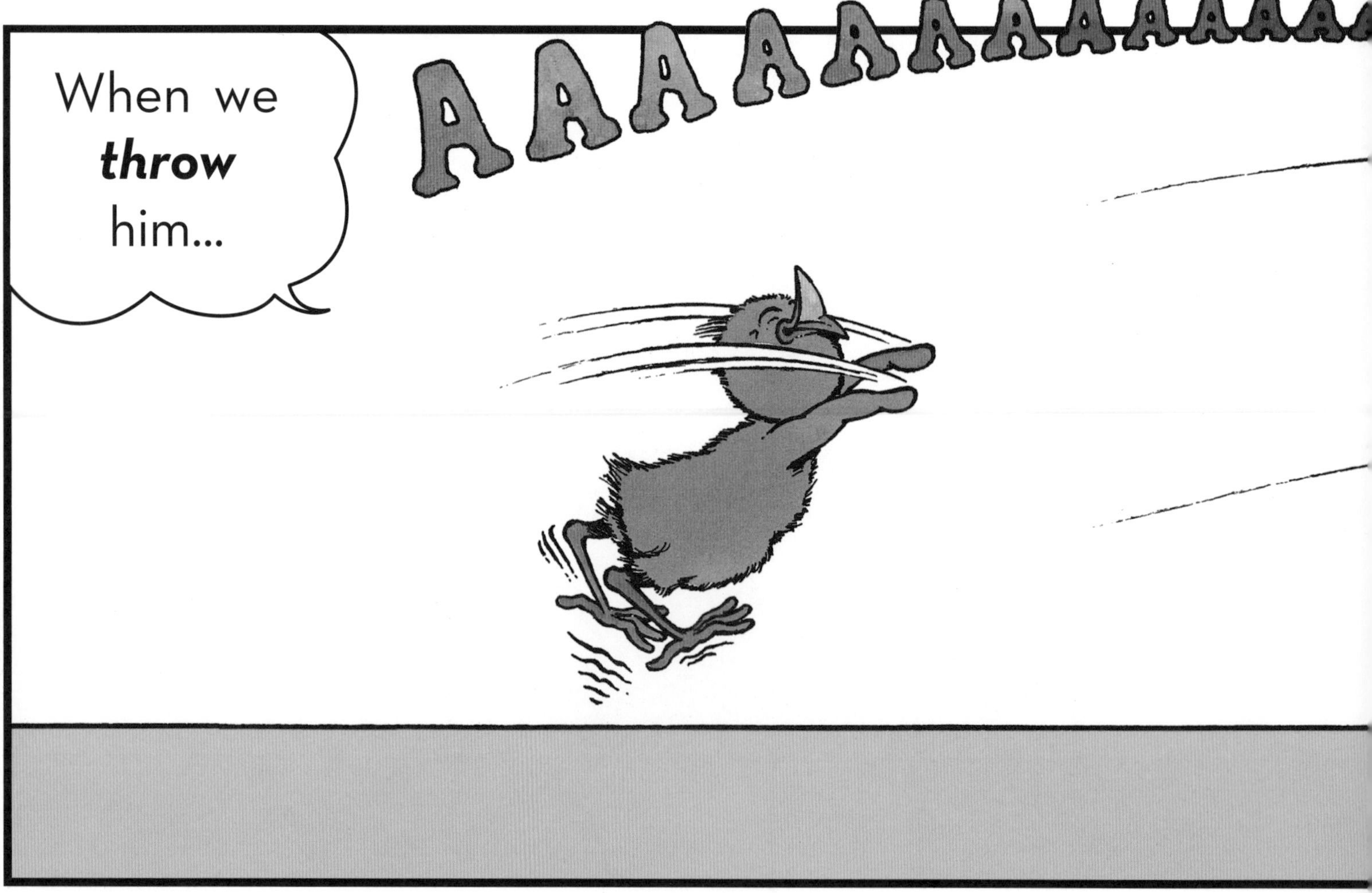
When we **throw** him...
AAAAAAAAAAAAA

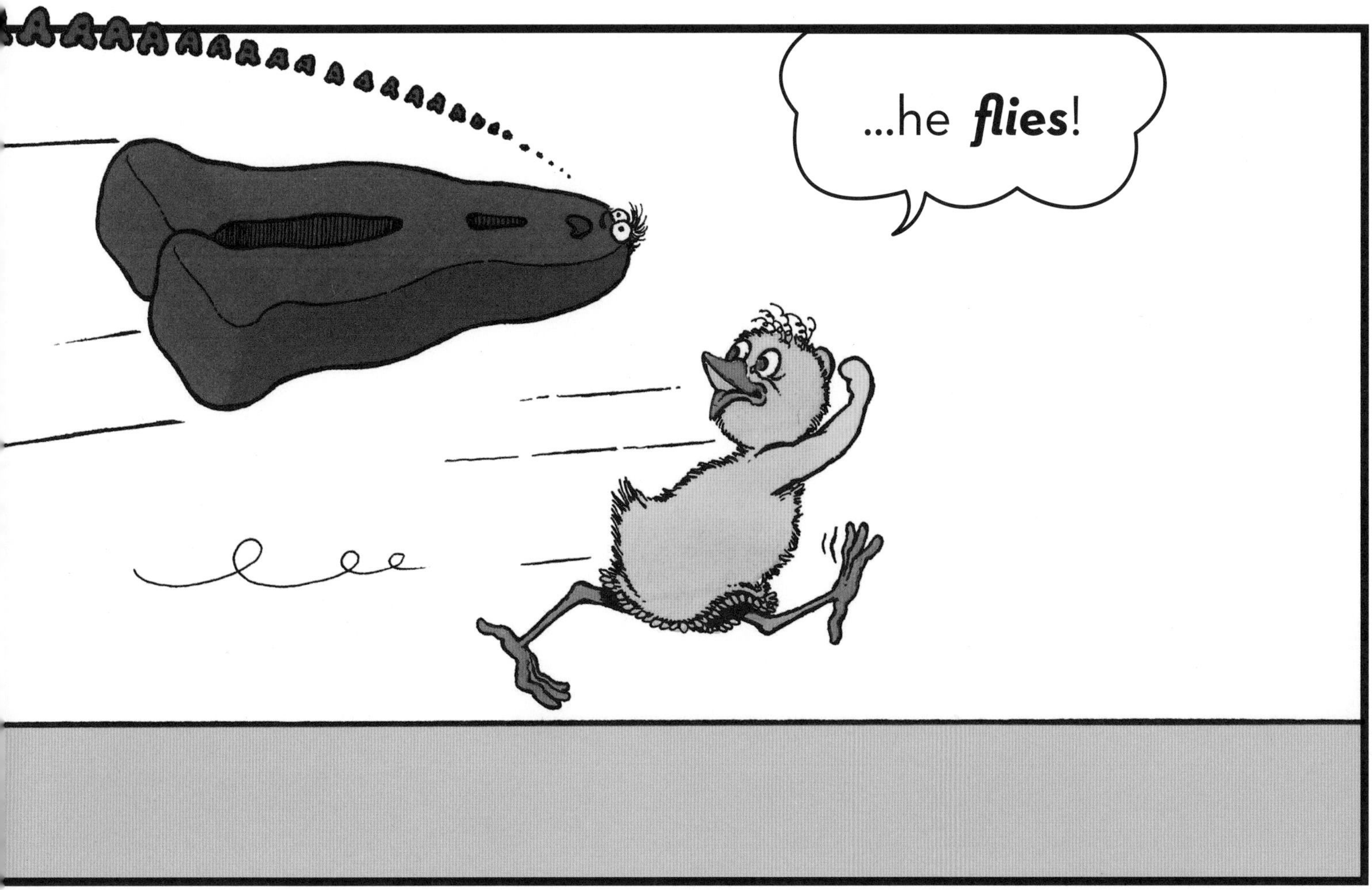
...he **flies**!

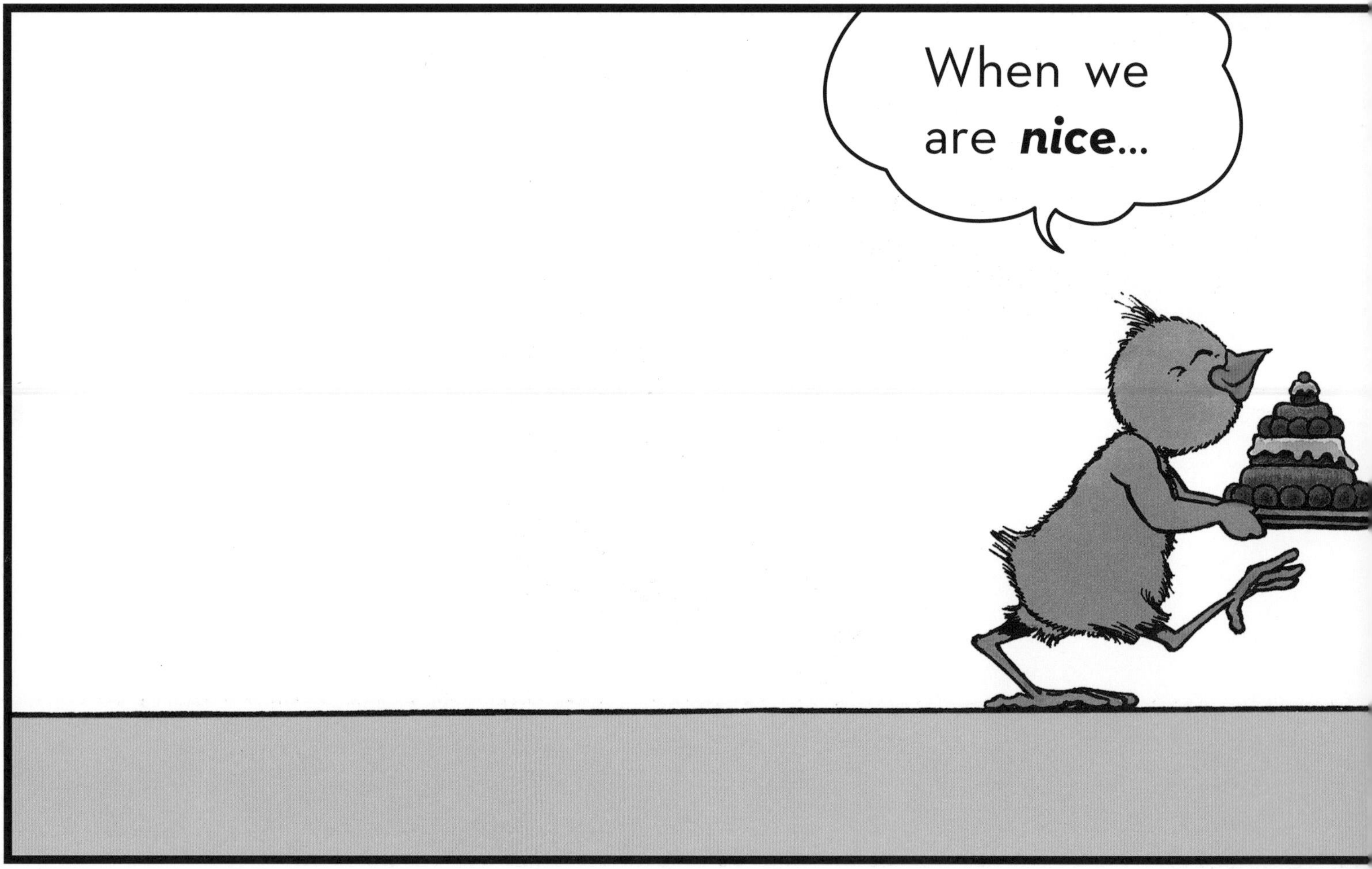
When we are **nice**...

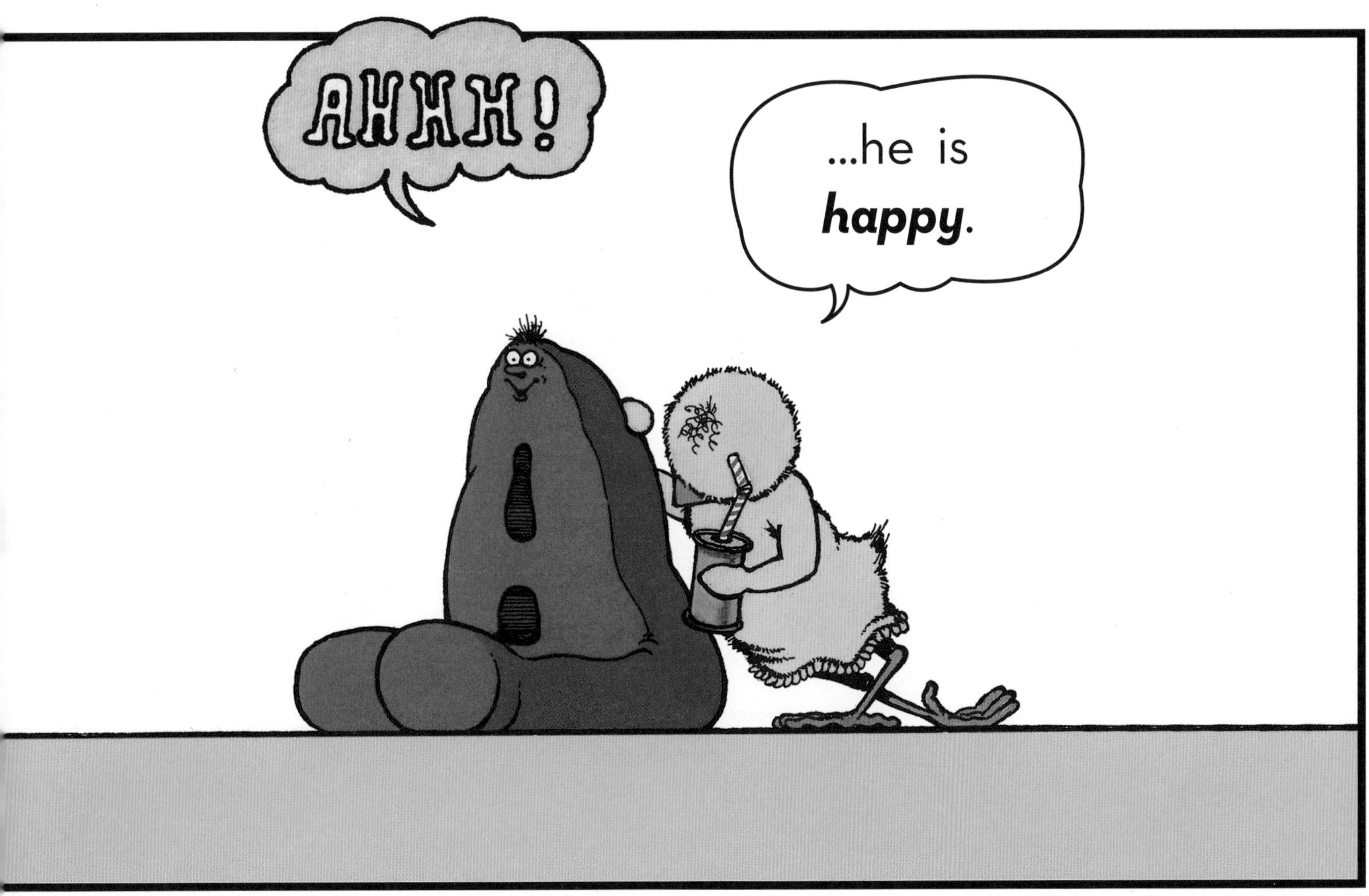
AHHH!
...he is **happy**.

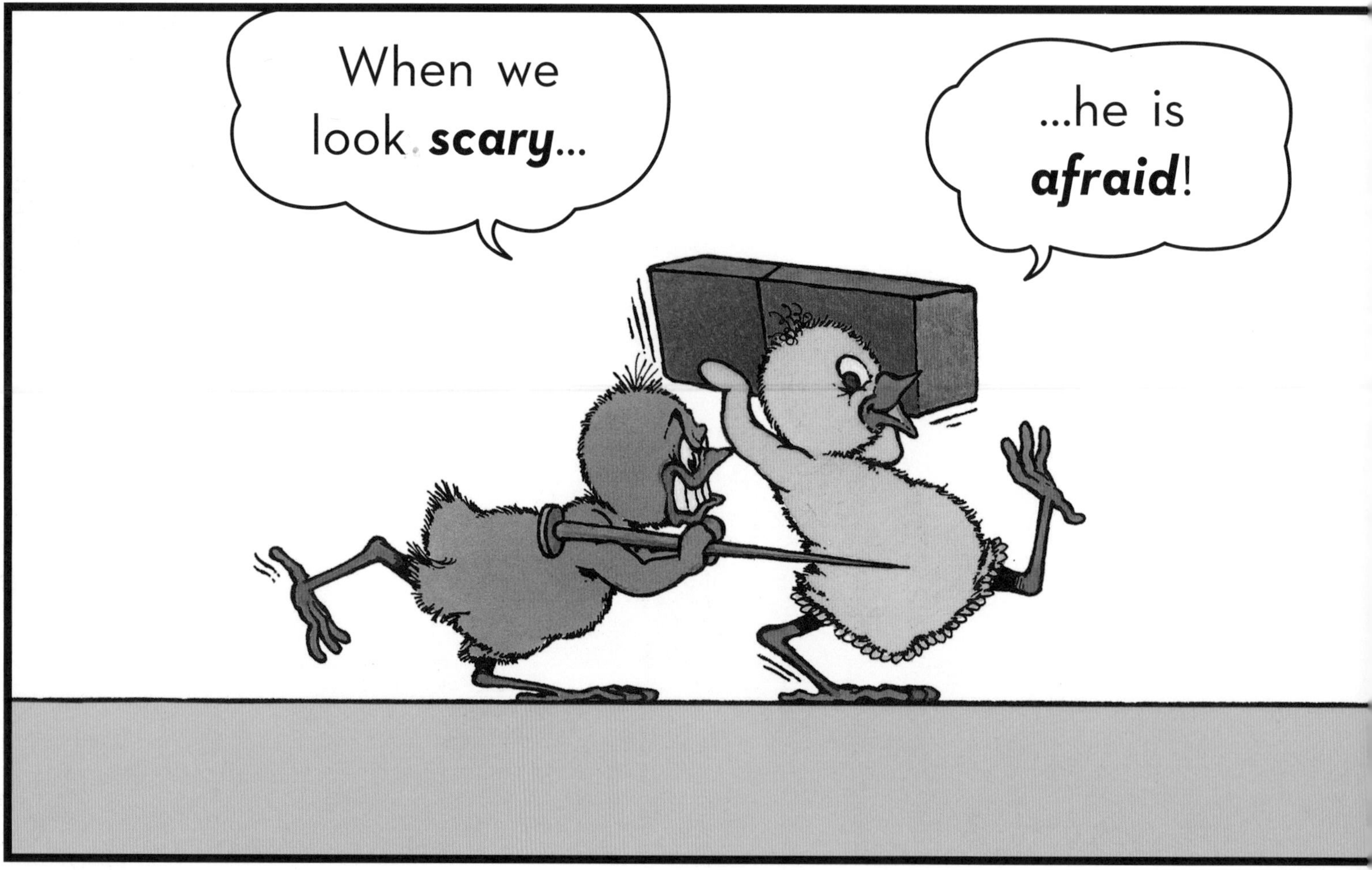
When we look **scary**...
...he is **afraid**!

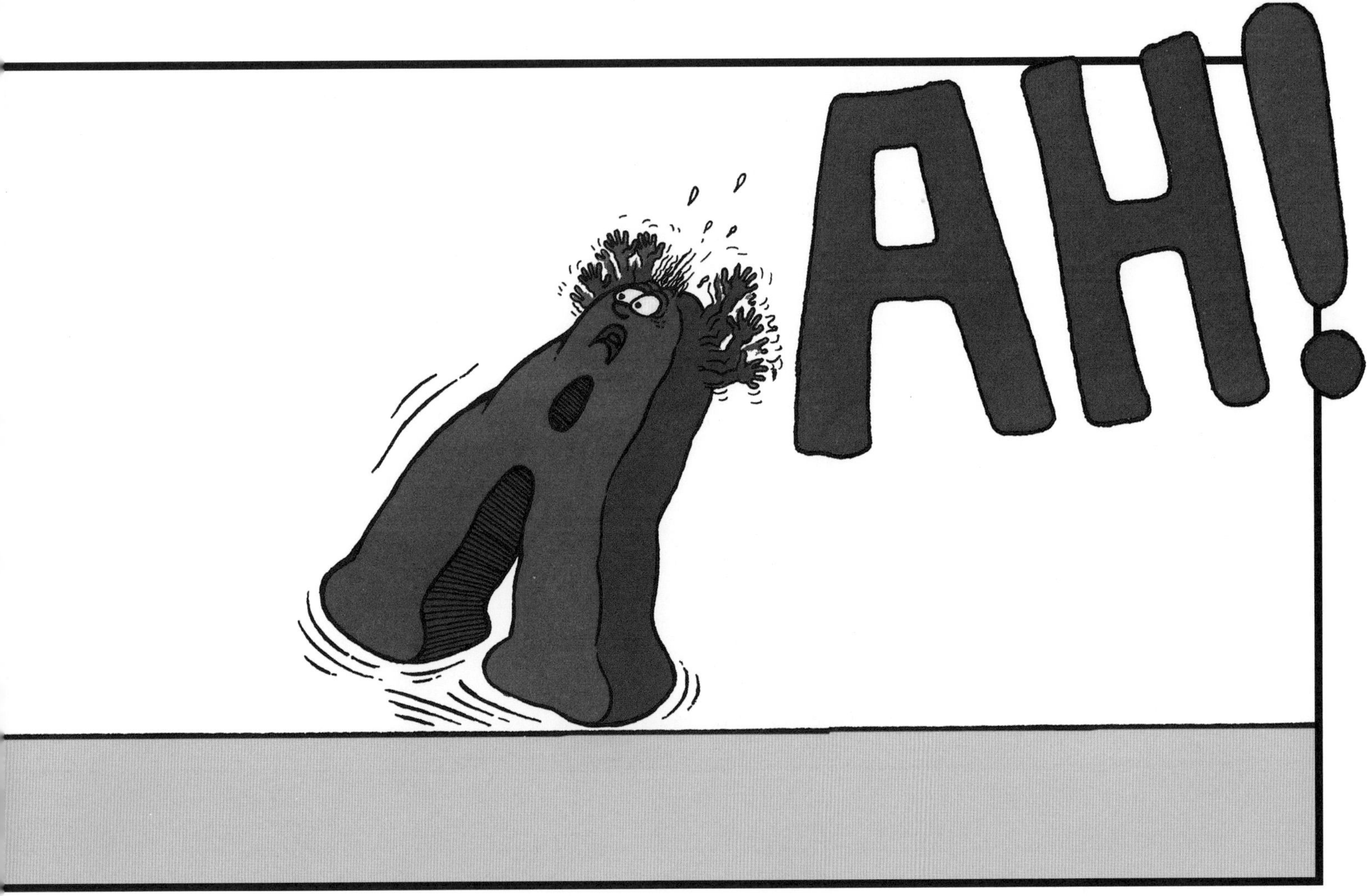
AH!

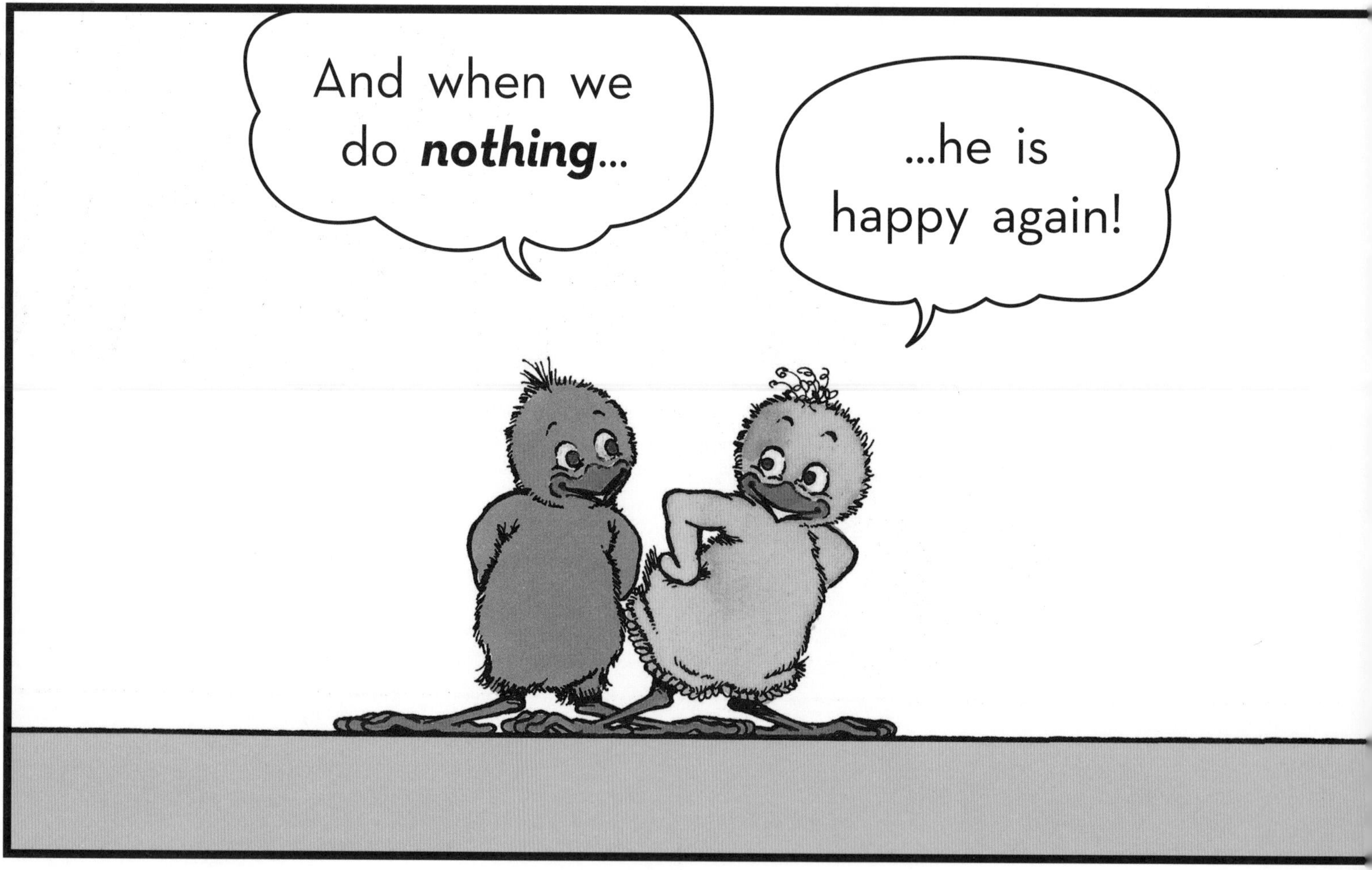
And when we do ***nothing***...
...he is happy again!

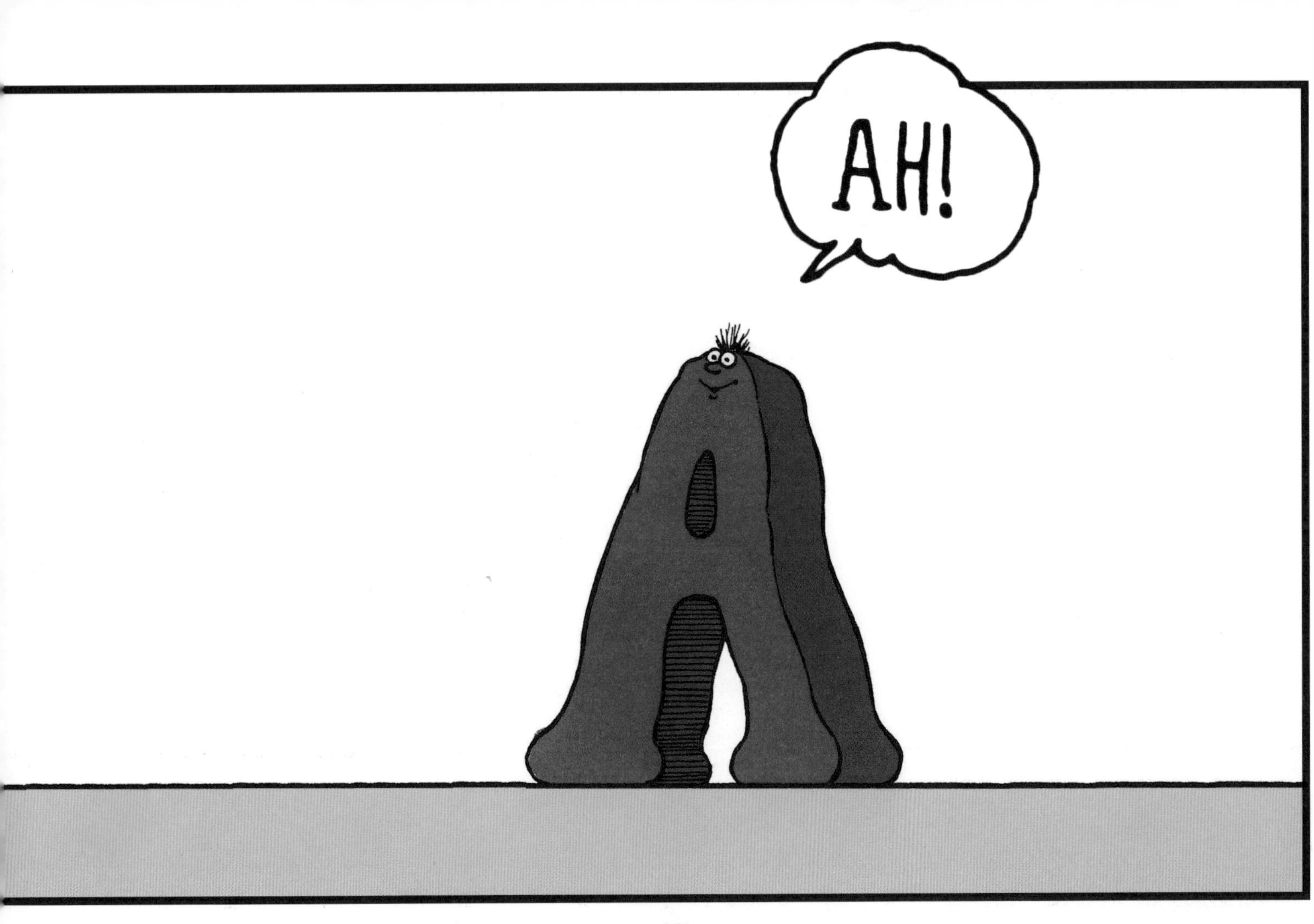
AH!

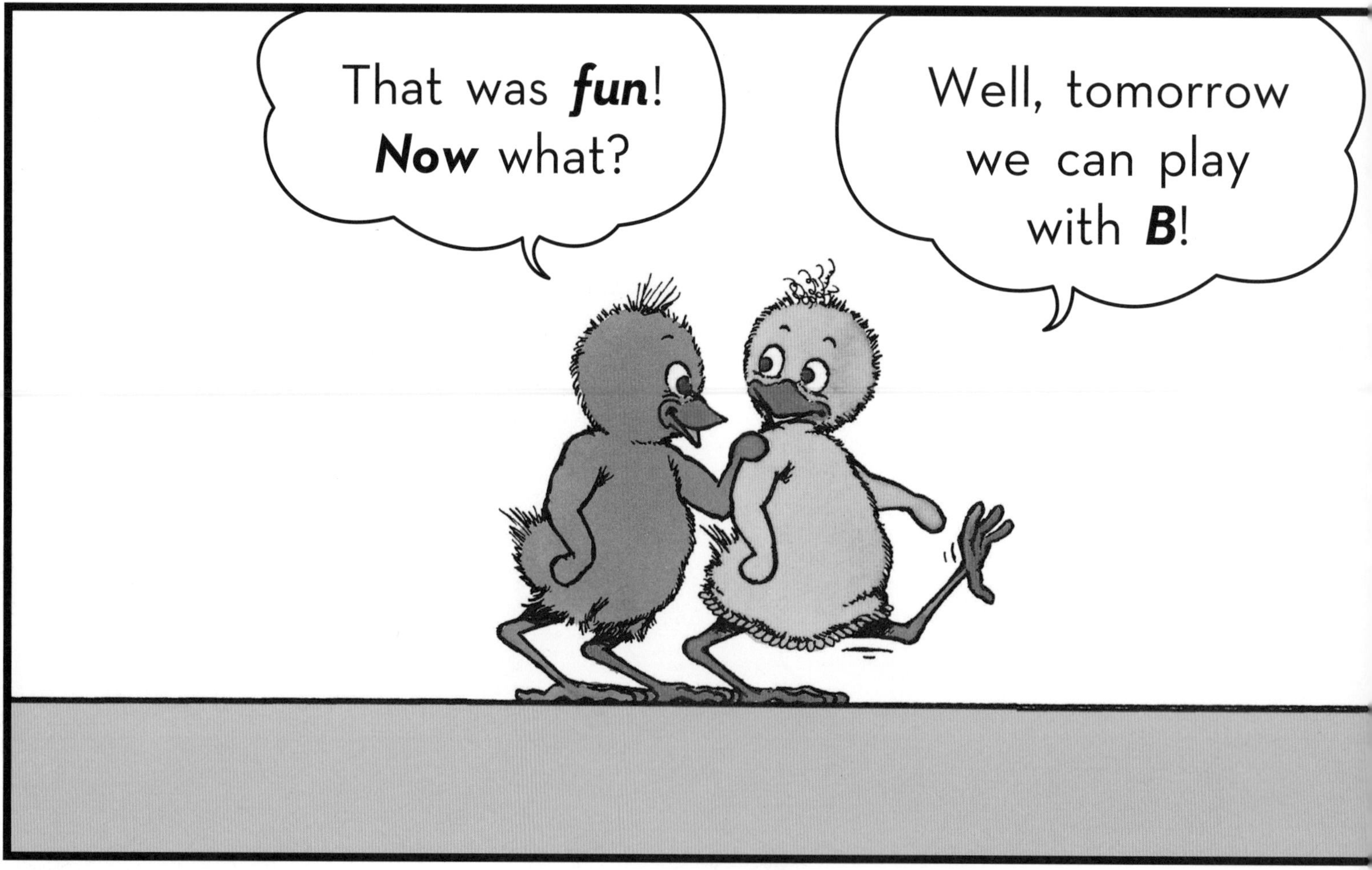
That was ***fun***! ***Now*** what?
Well, tomorrow we can play with ***B***!

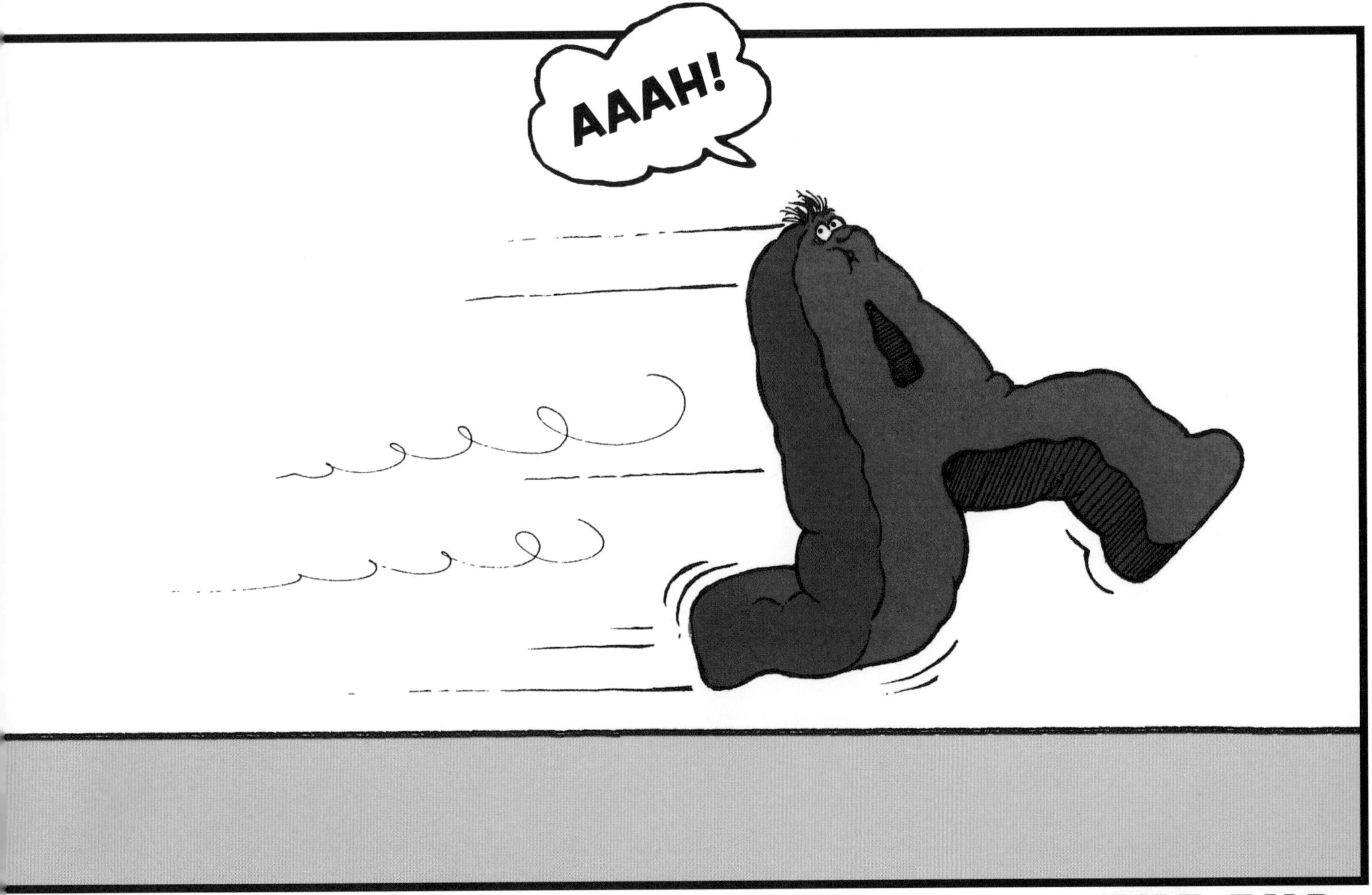
AAAH!

THE END

ABOUT THE AUTHOR

CLAUDE PONTI is a prolific author, painter and illustrator, beloved the world over for his humorous explorations of the nonsense world of dreams. The artist created his first picture book, *Adèle's Album,* to amuse his young daughter; he has since authored more than sixty children's books. On a personal note, Claude says: "I'm left-handed; I prefer cats to dogs (they don't lick people); and I'm not a vegetarian because I can't stand the cry of the lettuce or the carrot wrenched from the earth." He also fondly remembers climbing trees as a young boy, looking for the best spot to sit and read a book. He currently divides his time between the French countryside (where there are many birds, such as pheasants) and Paris (where there are pigeons).

HOW TO "TOON INTO READING"

in a few simple steps:

Our goal is to get kids reading—and we know kids LOVE comics. We publish award-winning early readers in comics form for elementary and early middle school, and present them in three levels.

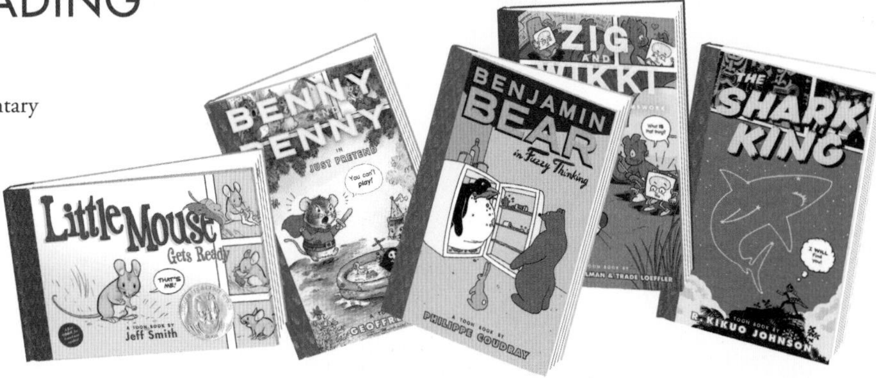

Little Mouse
Gets Ready
THAT'S ME!
A TOON BOOK BY
Jeff Smith
BENNY
IN
JUST PRETEND
You can't play!
BENJAMIN
BEAR
in Fuzzy Thinking
A TOON BOOK BY
PHILIPPE COUDRAY
ZIG
AND
THE
SHARK
KING
A TOON BOOK BY
R. KIKUO JOHNSON

1 FIND THE RIGHT BOOK

Veteran teacher Cindy Rosado tells what makes a good book for beginning and struggling readers alike: "A vetted vocabulary, plenty of picture clues, repetition, and a clear and compelling story. Also, the book shouldn't be too easy—or the reader won't learn, but neither should it be too hard—or he or she may get discouraged."

The TOON INTO READING!™ program is designed for beginning readers and works wonders with reluctant readers.

2 GUIDE YOUNG READERS

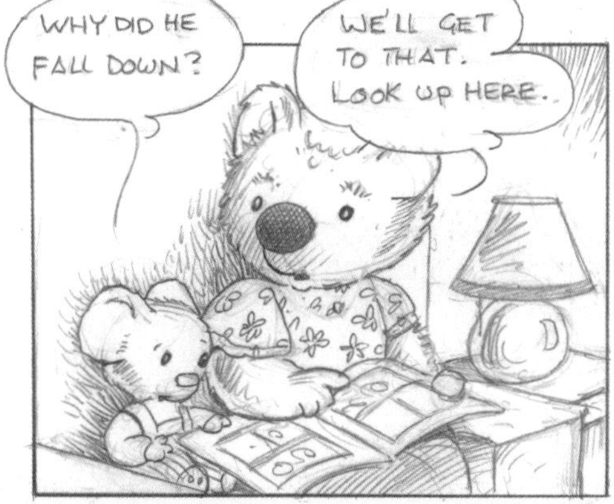

WHY DID HE FALL DOWN?
WE'LL GET TO THAT. LOOK UP HERE.

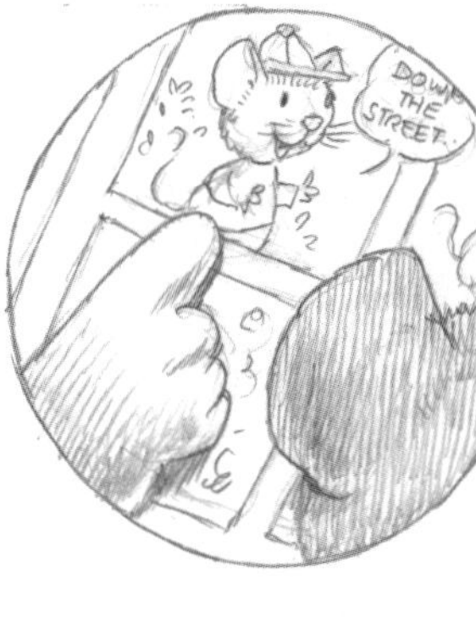

DOWN THE STREET.

What works?

Keep your fingertip <u>below</u> the character that is speaking.

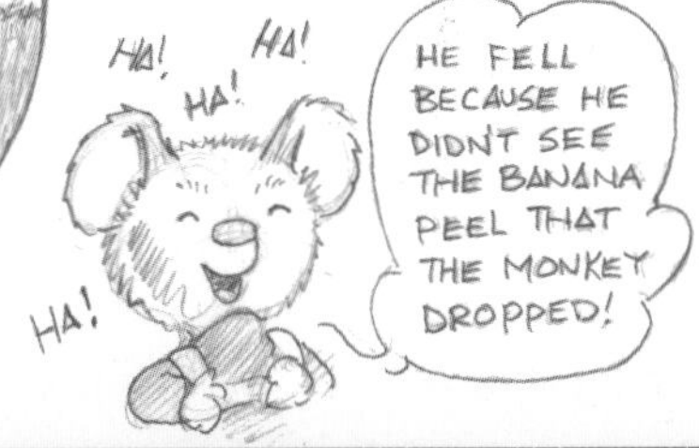

HA! HA! HA! HA!
HE FELL BECAUSE HE DIDN'T SEE THE BANANA PEEL THAT THE MONKEY DROPPED!

3 LET THEM GUESS

Comics provide a large amount of context for the words, so let young readers make informed guesses, and don't over-correct. In this panel, the artist shows a pirate ship, two pirate hats, and two pirate flags the first time the word "PIRATE" is introduced.

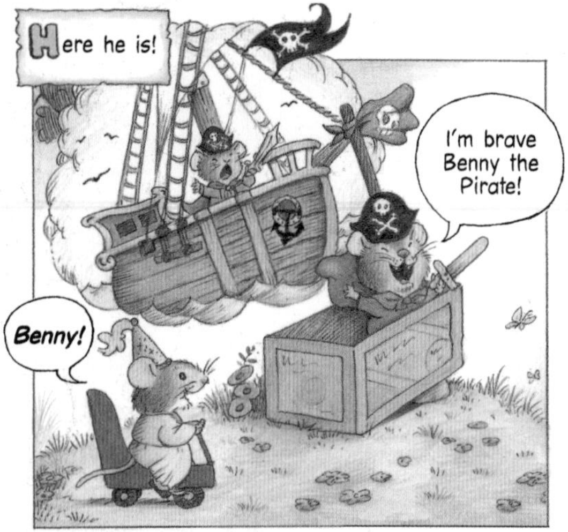
Here he is!
I'm brave Benny the Pirate!
Benny!

4 GET OUT THE CRAYONS

Kids see the hand of the author in a comic and it makes them want to tell their own stories. Encourage them to talk, write and draw!

5 TAKE TIME WITH SILENT PANELS

Comics use panels to mark time, and silent panels count. Look and "read" even when there are no words. Often, humor is all in the timing!

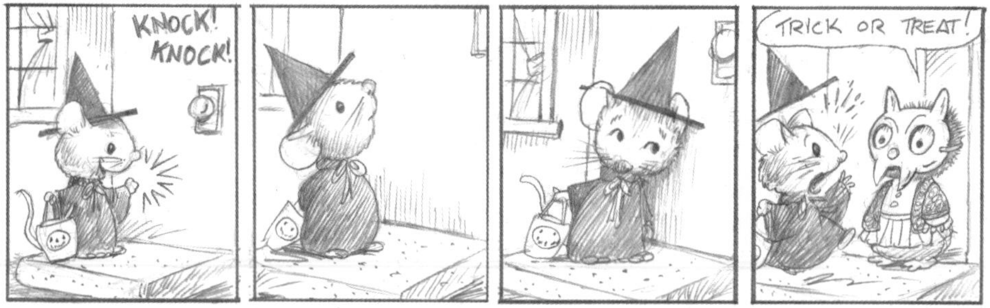
KNOCK! KNOCK!
TRICK OR TREAT!

6 HAVE FUN WITH BALLOONS

Comics use various kinds of balloons.

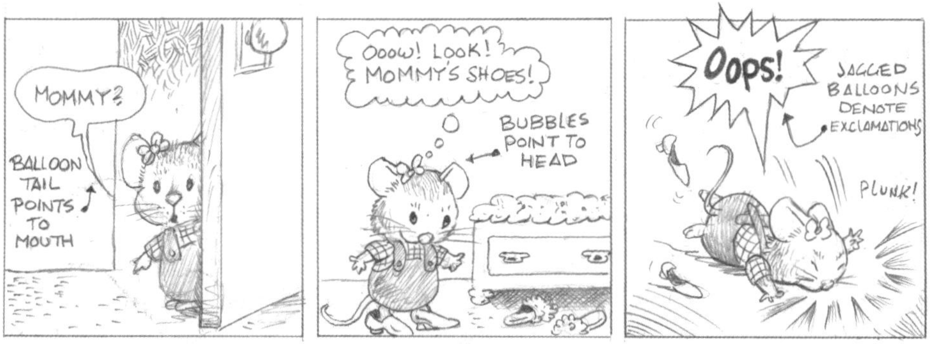
MOMMY?
BALLOON TAIL POINTS TO MOUTH
OOOW! LOOK! MOMMY'S SHOES!
BUBBLES POINT TO HEAD
Oops!
JAGGED BALLOONS DENOTE EXCLAMATIONS
PLUNK!

SPEECH BALLOONS THOUGHT BALLOONS SOUND EFFECTS